THE HAPPY LION'S QUEST

To Marc

Also by Louise Fatio and illustrated by Roger Duvoisin

THE HAPPY LION
THE HAPPY LION AND THE BEAR
THE HAPPY LION IN AFRICA
THE HAPPY LION ROARS
THE THREE HAPPY LIONS
A DOLL FOR MARIE
RED BANTAM

THE HAPPY LION'S QUEST

by LOUISE FATIO
illustrated by
ROGER DUVOISIN

McGraw-Hill Book Company New York • Toronto • London

The Happy Lion's Quest

The poor Happy Lion, how he sighed!
He sighed so loud, sitting in his house in the shaded zoo, that the lioness
said she could not sleep. He seemed so sad staring up into space looking
at nothing that his friends from town who came to say *bonjour* began to

worry. "Is our dear Happy Lion sick?" they asked. "Does he dream of jungles? Or is he very bored?"

How could the Happy Lion tell them he was dreaming of his dearest friend François, the keeper's son? How could he tell them he was sad because François was away at the *lycée* and would only come home for the vacations?

That was so far away. As far away as the *lycée*.

The sad Happy Lion, he so longed for his friend.

He would not eat. He would only stare and sigh.

"A friend is to visit, not to miss," he said with one last sigh. "Since François can't come and see me I must go and see him. That's very simple. I don't know why I didn't think of it before."

The Happy Lion went away that very night after saying goodbye to his wife and his son. He was not troubled about which road to take. "When one longs for a friend hard enough," he thought, "one just finds him."

He traveled all night straight across fields and slept during the next day in a deep wood. Hunger woke him up just as night fell, but that was nothing to worry about. When one is hungry one eats.

So, the Happy Lion ate. He lapped up two pailfuls of sour milk he found just inside a nearby barn. Two pails the farmer had left there for the pigs. It tasted so good the lion lapped to the bottom while the dog and the geese gave him a concert of barks and honks. The concert was so noisy the farmer came out and cried, "*Saperlipopette!* It's the Happy Lion who has escaped from the zoo. I must lock him up and call the police."

8

He tiptoed to the barn and — BANG!   He slammed the door with a kick.
"Tiens," said the lion, "the wind closed the door."   He tried to push it
but it was locked.   He felt the walls with his nose until he came to the
stable door.   The farmer had forgotten to lock it!   The lion pushed it
open and found himself among the cows.

"Bonsoir," he said.

"Bonsoir," said the cows in unison.

At the far end of the stable the Happy Lion saw the bright stars through a
large opening.   It was the door to the barnyard.   Wide open!

"Well," said the lion as he went out, "that was a nice meal," and began his trek across pastures.

It was just before dawn that he saw a little wiggling light on a lonely stretch of road — the light from *gendarme* Pépin's bicycle. *Le gendarme* was on his way home after hunting lions all night. "Ah, *zut!*" he cried, "here comes the Happy Lion, and I left my gun at the *poste de police*. I could have made some noises with it."

Le gendarme threw his bike in a ditch and ran to the nearest tree. "One never knows with lions," he said. "When he's gone I'll give the alarm."

"I'm glad that man is gone," thought the Happy Lion. "One never knows with men when they are not at the zoo." And feeling tired now, he went to stretch under *gendarme* Pépin's tree for a good day's sleep.

That's why *le gendarme* Pépin was up in the tree all day. If he moved a leg the lion pricked an ear, so he never dared climb down. When evening came he was so tired he fell asleep in a crotch, and it was just then that the Lion woke up and walked away.

Of course, the Happy Lion was hungry again. But his meal was not far
off. As he approached an abandoned truck in a narrow forest road, he
smelled meat. He climbed into the truck through the open upper door at
the back, and there, behind a bale of hay, he found a bundle of the finest
meat, the same kind he had at the zoo every day.
The Happy Lion became so busy with his dinner he did not hear footsteps

at the front of the truck.   Before he could jump out, the motor roared and the truck was on its way.

"Well, it was a mistake to climb up here," he worried.   "Now, where am I going?"   But it was not a mistake at all, really.   The truck was going in the right direction.   It was driven by Monsieur Boudin, the farmer, who sat in company with two *gendarmes*.   And where were they going? . . .   Oh, they were on their way to seek the Happy Lion — seek him in all the places where he had "been seen" at the same time!   The meat in the back? Why, it was to lure the lion if they found him!   The truck rolled along for such

a long time that the roar-roar-roar of its motor put the Happy Lion to sleep. It was a sleep so deep he did not hear when the truck stopped near a ruined castle.

"Someone saw something here that had a lion's tail," whispered a *gendarme.* "Let's go and take a look."

"Watch out," warned Monsieur Boudin; "don't get too near."

The *gendarmes* crawled round one side of the castle whispering to one another and came out the other side calling very loud:

"It's a donkey's tail!"

Then Monsieur Boudin drove to a very old bridge "where the mailman saw the Happy Lion taking an afternoon nap."
Then to a low farmhouse "where the farmer's wife saw him bathing in the pond."   And to a pinewood "where an old woman said he ran after her."
They searched inside a crumbling tower; behind haystacks; in ditches and behind old walls; wherever "the lion was seen."

They drove on all night. But there was no Happy Lion.
"That lion is very clever," said Monsieur Boudin toward morning. "He is everywhere and he is nowhere."
The sun was high in the sky when they parked the truck in a small town with cobbled streets. They wanted to have breakfast and they wanted to talk about where the Happy Lion could be.

As soon as the motor became still, the Happy Lion woke up. "I must have
been asleep," he yawned. "Where am I?" While the three men jumped
down one side of the truck, he jumped down at the back and found himself

near a high wrought-iron gate with the word *LYCÉE* written at the top.
The Happy Lion did not need to read to know he had arrived. That was
clear. There were boys playing soccer in the yard and three professors

talking in the shade of a tree.   He walked in.

"Oh, la, la, look who comes here.   *UN LION!*" cried the three professors, and climbed up the tree in a hurry.

"It's the Happy Lion, for sure," cried the boys.

"IT'S FRANÇOIS' HAPPY LION!"

"Let's take him to François in Monsieur Balet's class," said a boy as the three professors climbed down the tree. "Will he be glad to see the Happy Lion!"

When Monsieur Balet heard a knock at his door he put down his glasses and said very loud, *"ENTREZ."* The Happy Lion did.

What a scuffle and a hubbub!

"MY HAPPY LION!" cried François, running over to his friend.

"*VIVE* the Happy Lion!" cried the whole class.

"*SILENCE!*" cried Monsieur Balet.

"My poor dear Happy Lion," said François, hugging his friend tight. "That's why you ran away. It was to see me. I was so worried when I read it in the newspapers."

"I knew I would find him if I wished it hard enough," thought the Happy Lion, rubbing his nose against François.

But Monsieur Balet kept striking his ruler on his desk, louder and louder, and shouted, "*SILENCE!* Everyone to his seat. I will not be interrupted when I talk and give a *leçon!*"

There was a rush and a hush. All sat, even the lion, who did so on François' bench. And so, for the first time the Happy Lion had a *leçon* in *arithmétique*. He sat very still.

Monsieur Balet was so pleased the lion would listen so quietly that he said when the class was over, *"François, mon garçon*, I'll give you a holiday to take your friend home."

"O, merci bien, monsieur."

"Wait, and I'll even drive you myself in my little automobile."

There was joy in the Happy Lion's home town when Monsieur Balet's car arrived. The band was waiting at the town gate with its trombones and drums, the flags waved over the roofs, and *Monsieur le Maire* read a beautiful speech about friendship.

François received permission to come home every week end so the Happy Lion would never remain so long without seeing him. And that made the lioness and her son happy too; not only because they loved François but because, as the lioness said:

"My dear Happy Lion is such poor company when he misses François."